The Capacity to Serve and Other Stories

Simon Christiansen

Copyright © 2023 Simon Christiansen

All rights reserved.

ISBN: 978-87-94505-00-0

DEDICATION

This book is dedicated to my family and friends, who gave me invaluable feedback on the stories, and to those editors who originally accepted them for publication.

This collection would not exist without you.

CONTENTS

THE CAPACITY TO SERVE

Penguins are tiny tuxedo-clad dwarven butlers, looking deceptively fit to serve, but with two useless flippers, incapable of carrying even a simple tray with a cup of tea and maybe a bowl of Turkish delight.

Their lack of opposable thumbs infuriated me.

My grandmother owned two penguins. Rare emperor breeds that waddled through the winding passageways of her home, looking for fish, which she often hid in nooks and crannies around the old mansion.

As I tried to sleep, I listened to their feet shuffling through the halls outside.

Shuffle.

Shuffle.

Shuffle.

Fish.

My grandmother lived in the country. Far from the lights of the city. Far from my friends. Far from fun. My parents insisted that I visit her during the summer. I was bored without my toys and friends. She had one thing we didn't have in the city, though.

The penguins. Very few city folks kept penguins. They didn't like the noise. It was hard to keep your home at an appropriate temperature, with the thermostat controlled by Central Heating, and the light by the sun.

Most people who could afford penguins moved to the country. In the country, you could do whatever you wanted.

The short one was named Martin; the tall one, Copernicus.

I helped them find the fish that my grandmother hid around the mansion. Once found, I threw the fish into the air, the penguins craned their necks back, and the fish disappeared down their throats without a sound. Like shadows swallowed by the night.

Once I learned my grandmother's habits, the fish became easy to find. The penguins were happy to receive their food, but I grew bored. I started to hide fish myself, choosing more challenging locations, prolonging the playtime.

Once, I hid a fish inside a suit of armour in the grand hall, and the penguins vanquished the empty knight. The different pieces of the armour split apart. The helmet rolled out the front door, down the stone steps of the front stairs. The penguins ate the fish while my grandmother castigated me and made me put the armour back together.

Hiding the fish put me in a position of authority over the penguins. It wasn't long before I stopped thinking of them as friends. I started seeing them as servants, delivering fun rather than participating as equals.

I wanted them to serve more directly. I procured a tray from the kitchen, decorating it with a nice cup of hot tea and a bowl of Turkish delight. My grandmother always had plenty, and it did look very colourful.

"Copernicus," I called. "Wanna play a new game?"

Copernicus waddled to my side. Martin was still sleeping in

his basket in the corner of the room.

I instructed Copernicus to bend his flipper. The penguin seemed nonplussed at this strange game. Martin raised his head and watched from his basket.

Copernicus bent the flipper as requested and looked at it, as if expecting a fish to materialize on the smooth surface. I took the tray from the table, carried it to the large penguin, and placed it on top of the bent flipper. It stayed.

Instructing Copernicus to keep perfectly still, I returned to the easy chair at the other end of the room.

"OK, Copernicus," I said. "Bring me the tray."

Copernicus waddled one step forward. The tray slid from his flipper and crashed to the floor. The teacup broke, tea soaking into the carpet. The Turkish delight bounced everywhere, a rain of multicoloured gels.

"What the fuck was the point of that?" said Copernicus.

"He is distracting us," said Martin from his basket. "While he hides the fish."

"Guys," I said. "I am trying to help you become more useful."

"We are eminently useful at eliminating the fish surplus," proclaimed Copernicus.

"You need to be useful to humans, the providers of fish. Your natural habitats are long gone, remember? If we don't give you fish, no one will."

"Give me a fish, then," said Copernicus. "Or you are not useful to us."

I sighed and tossed him a lantern fish. Its huge eye stared at me as it soared through the air. It disappeared into the darkness within Copernicus's beak.

Martin made that sound penguins make, and I threw him a herring.

***

Copernicus liked jazz. Sometimes, when the rain was pounding against the windows, we would sit in the drawing-room listening to Oscar Peterson and Niels-Henning Ørsted Pedersen. Martin preferred progressive rock, not the best choice for a rainy afternoon.

One day, while I was close to dozing off in the drawing-room easy chair, Copernicus asked me if I had ever heard of the Great Auk.

"The great orc? Like, Uruk-hai?"

"The Great Auk. It's a bird, like Martin and me."

"Can't say that I have."

"The Great Auk, or Pinguinus impennis, was a flightless bird, which became extinct in the nineteenth century. We modern penguins are named after our resemblance to this bird, even though there is no close relation. We are the shadows cast on the cave wall by the Great Auk, the last true Pinguinus."

The smooth piano and bass music flowing from the radio mingled with my thoughts as I tried to think of an answer.

Copernicus continued: "The Great Auk was hunted to extinction for its feathers, which were used to make pillows. By 1835, fewer than fifty birds survived, hiding on the small island of Eldey. They did not survive for long. In June 1840, Jón Brandsson and Sigurður Ísleifsson strangled the last pair of Auks in the world, acting on behalf of a private collector. Their friend, Ketill Ketilsson, smashed the last remaining Auk egg with his boot."

"Why are you telling me this?"

"So you will know that we remember."

The jazz filled the silence between us.

***

Further experiments in servitude yielded results no better than the first. The penguins were incapable of using their flippers to carry anything at all. They were like Teflon; nothing stuck.

Years passed. I lived my life at home. Played with the penguins when visiting my grandmother. Dreamed of dominance. The penguins were subservient, sure, but what good is subservience without the capacity to serve?

When I reached my teens, I stopped visiting my grandmother as often, spending most of my time in the city.

At college, I studied biology. At first on a theoretical level, but my studies eventually drifted towards biomodification. I didn't want to know what animals were like; I wanted to decide.

It was during my studies at the University of Copenhagen that I hatched my plan. I carried the idea in my mind for months as it developed, like a male emperor penguin incubating his egg.

I threw myself into my studies. While other students partied, I experimented on mice, parrots, platypuses and echidnas. My thesis project was a mouse with the beak of a parrot, standing on two legs, on platypus flippers. It could repeat a few simple words. It lived for two weeks.

I moved away from such extravagance, shifting my focus to improving animals in more subtle ways. I designed a corgi that could walk on its hind legs, a giraffe that could blend with its surroundings like a chameleon, avoiding predators, and a cat with eleven lives and two tails.

I became well known in the biomod community, without ever achieving any real fame. My work was, after all, not as crowd-pleasing as more ostentatious projects, such as Dr. Christianson's renowned omni-dog.

When I was ready, I called my grandmother to reminisce about the old days. She was still in good health, as were her penguins. She was a wealthy woman and could afford to maintain her body and those of her loved ones.

We decided I should come visit the next fortnight. We could all catch up, my grandmother, the penguins and I.

In a fit of nostalgia, I wiped the dust off my old backpack and went down to the fishmonger's. The neon mackerel above the automated doors soaked me in blue light. Inside, I filled the backpack with lantern fish, krill, crustaceans and a veritable cornucopia of cephalopods. I needed the penguins on my side for my plan to proceed.

"Wow, you own a penguin?" asked the girl behind the counter, a short brunette.

"My grandmother does," I said. "She lives in the country, so I'm bringing some treats for the penguins when I visit."

Her eyes widened when she recognized the plurality. "My dad owned a little blue, but he couldn't afford the mortgage on it, in the end."

Soon, penguins would be able to earn their existence.

I stored the fish in a backpack cooler, entered my Bentley and told it to take me to my grandmother. It still remembered the way, after all these years.

As the sun set behind the horizon, the mansion loomed before me, ancient as always.

The car stuttered and came to a halt in the driveway.

My grandmother appeared in the doorway. She was wearing a light-blue Indian salwar suit, as was the current fashion among wealthy women. She seemed to float down the steps with precise movements.

"Grandmother," I said. "You have not changed."

She shrugged. "Change is for the poor. I can afford to stay the same. You have grown a lot, though."

"I have yet to reach the age where permanence becomes desirable."

We went inside and walked through the winding halls of the mansion. In the distance, I could hear the shuffling of the penguins.

We entered the drawing-room. The same easy chair was still there. I sat down without asking. My grandmother took the couch.

"I understand that you have made a name for yourself in the biomod community," said my grandmother.

"A small name," I said, sipping my brandy. "But a name, yes."

"I have never been much interested in biomodification," said my grandmother. "For sure, the omni-dog is an interesting creation, but I prefer my penguins."

"I understand," I said. "Where are the penguins, anyway?"

"They are coming. Listen for the shuffling of their feet."

"You must admit," I said, "that the penguins are quite useless in their current form. I enjoy their company as much as you but imagine if they could carry a tray with tea and snacks. Wouldn't that be wonderful?"

She yawned. "That does sound nice. I suppose you're proposing some form of biomodification?"

"I am."

She was quiet for a bit. "If the penguins want it, who am I to refuse them? You will make your case to them."

I heard shuffling outside the door to the drawing-room.

The door creaked open, and Martin and Copernicus entered the room.

They called my name from the open door, and I smiled.

As they gained the centre of the room, I reached into my backpack cooler and produced two perfect, wide-eyed lantern fish.

With a flip of my wrist, the fish sailed through the air and disappeared down the throats of the two penguins.

"Nice to see you still have it," I told them.

"I could say the same," said Copernicus. "Nice backhand."

"I have a proposition for you," I continued. "Catching fish with your mouths is great, but what if you could pick them up with your flippers? You wouldn't need humans to throw the fish anymore."

"We would need humans to catch the fish," said Martin.

Copernicus was quicker on the uptake. "Not necessarily. Penguins used to catch fish by ourselves, in the before time. With more flexible flippers, we could carry a fish in each flipper and another in the mouth."

"Three fish to a penguin!" cried Martin.

I asked my aunt if I could use her basement, and she concurred.

***

The basement was a labyrinth, a combined library and wine cellar. A huge, cavernous dome with alternating wine- and bookshelves superimposed on rock walls. A large round mahogany table in the centre. Light from a sparkling chandelier hanging from the rocky ceiling. Its central hall was perfect for my purposes.

I popped open a Château Cheval Blanc 1947 and took a sip straight from the bottle. "Let's get this party started."

Copernicus might have liked to answer, but he was bound

and gagged in the centre of the table, his consent recorded and stored in the cloud for posterity. I could see the sedative starting to take hold. He struggled to keep his eyes open, looking at me with a mixture of curiosity and fear.

His eyes closed. I never knew penguins could snore.

I retrieved my tools from my bag on the stone floor. Gleaming, sharpened spinkifiers, cartwailers and scrivs soon covered the table. To an untrained eye, mere pieces of stainless steel bent into abstract shapes. To a trained biomodificationist, the tools of the art.

Copernicus first, then Martin.

***

I sat on a plain wooden chair, sipping the last of the wine and reading a signed first edition of Tamerlane, when the penguins started moving, awakening.

They were no longer restrained. I put away the bottle and book.

Slowly, both penguins got to their feet, shuffling from side to side on the table, the sedative still in their blood.

They both jumped to the floor and steadied themselves.

"Fish?" said Martin.

"Soon," I replied.

From a small table by a wall, I procured a delicate round tray holding several cups and plates of the finest china, as well as a small raku bowl of Turkish delight. I filled the cups with hot tea and supported the tray with my right hand.

The penguins hesitated. Copernicus stepped forward.

He lifted his right flipper. At first, it looked no different than before. Then small cracks appeared in the smooth black surface, and the flipper split into five segments, undulating independently in the air.

I placed the tray on the five flipper sections, which moved to support the surface. The tray stayed perfectly level.

Penguin tentacles.

Pentacles.

***

The penguins carried the trays up and down stairs, through doorways, down long winding corridors, up rickety ladders, even down a makeshift water slide I constructed in the great hall.

The pentacles proved even more efficient than human hands, adjusting their positions to keep the trays perfectly level, the surface of the tea completely undisturbed, like a quiet pond reflecting the moon.

I smiled.

My grandmother and I indulged in gallons of Earl Grey and piles of Turkish delight.

As the penguins delivered their trays, their pentacles would extend, smoothly extracting fish from my cooler bag in the corner. I allowed this, relishing the fact that the penguins were becoming self-maintaining servants.

I sipped my tea and presented my proposal to my grandmother. "How do you like your new servants?"

She sipped her tea as well and chose a bluish-green piece of Turkish delight. "I must confess, it is refreshing to have such capable help."

"Many other people would feel the same way," I said. "Many people possess penguins; few find them useful. That could change. All it takes is funding."

My grandmother wasn't stupid. She had already written the

cheque.

***

With my skills and her money, we developed a diverse stable of emperors, kings, fairies, chinstraps, magellanics and macaronis.

Soon, the mansion was abuzz with every imaginable penguin carrying out every imaginable task. Some carried trays, but others swept the floors, painted the walls, washed the car, cooked dinner and even typed simple letters on my grandmother's old electric typewriter.

Everywhere you looked, you saw undulating pentacles engaged in useful tasks.

My grandmother and I held our meetings in the drawing-room, planning our next moves. Penguins brought us tea, food, Turkish delight and whatever else we requested.

We sold our first penguin to my grandmother's neighbour. Dr. Jørgensen lived only a few miles away, in a smaller mansion near the woods. His arthritis had been getting worse for years and he was dependent on a visiting nurse to help with everyday chores. The travel time was long, and the nurse couldn't come very often. He was considering selling the house.

He had a cat named Cornelius, but it was if anything even less useful than a normal penguin.

We introduced him to a well-spoken macaroni named Matheo, who combed back the yellow crest on his head with his pentacles while he took stock of the place. He and the professor exchanged a few pleasantries, and the penguin went to work.

"I don't like it, Doc," said Cornelius the cat. "It makes the rest of us look bad in comparison."

Matheo opened a can of tuna, and Cornelius stopped complaining.

Word spread like wildfire. In less than a week we had sold most of our stock to the locals. In less than two weeks we could pick and choose between the business propositions.

Casper Mortensen himself came to visit us, arriving in his trademark blue vintage Bell 47 helicopter. It is not every day the president of the second largest biomod pet store in the country drops by.

He jumped from the chopper to the patio, twirling his bright blue moustache. He was wearing pinstripes, and his tie was dark grey with a stylized DNA pattern.

"I want to sell your penguins," he said, seconds after landing on the tiles, the dust still settling around his jet-black spring boots.

"Would you like tea?" asked my grandmother.

He nodded. "Let me see what they can do."

Pentacled penguins brought trays of tea, snacks, Turkish delight, and bananas. They balanced the cups, trays and snacks on the table, while an adorable blue fairy penguin peeled the bananas.

In less than a minute the table was set. While the penguins twirled their pentacles, Casper Mortensen twirled his blue moustache.

He took a single sip of his tea, then threw the cup on the ground in a display of dominance. The fine china splintered into a thousand pieces.

"I will have my people prepare the papers." He bounced back into the helicopter, which sped off into the sunset.

***

Whereas before, penguins had been status symbols for the idle rich, now they became biological household appliances. Casper Mortensen's company increased production and penguin prices fell to the point where a basic pentacled chinstrap barely cost more than a used Ford Fiesta.

Soon, penguins were everywhere. Butlers, bartenders, housemaids, firefighters, drivers, nurses, ticket-sellers and hotdog vendors. From the most useless animal to the most practical.

I took the one o'clock hypercube to Copenhagen Central to get to my new offices in the Mortensen tower. Casper Mortensen himself picked me up on the first day. A 3D projection of the cube rotated slowly above the station as we exchanged pleasantries.

Casper Mortensen presented me with a pair of brand-new black Eshington spring boots. As the new head of the biomod department, I would have to move with style. We bounced down the street together towards the tower.

From my office near the top floor, I could see the entire city of Copenhagen stretched out beneath me, like a miniature play-set ripe for the conquest. I smiled. A penguin brought me tea. I drank.

"I will improve you," I said.

***

I busied myself with my work. In the extensive biomod labs of the Mortensen Corporation, my assistants and I tweaked and improved the penguin procedures. We made their pentacles ever more flexible and precise, to the point where a single pentacle could split a human hair in twain.

After a few years, my grandmother invited me home for a

short vacation. She had been happy to stay out of the day-to-day operations of the penguin business, collecting the dividends from her mansion. Martin and Copernicus were still living with her, now as her servants.

I took the hypercube to Vojens, and my car brought me the rest of the way there. The car now had a driver: a king penguin wearing a dark-blue Stetson cap. Penguin prices had dropped to the point where a penguin driver was cheaper than maintaining the auto-car component. I kind of missed my old auto-car, but the penguin was well trained, and we passed the time discussing recent events.

The car stopped in front of the mansion a little after five o'clock. I stepped out onto the gravel and fetched my backpack from the trunk. The car sped away. I hadn't told the penguin to leave me, but I figured it knew what it was doing.

I stood there for a few minutes, waiting for my grandmother to come greet me. The air was cool, but the fading light from the sun still kept me warm.

I walked up to the door and knocked. The knocks echoed in the hallway inside. There was no answer. I turned the knob and went inside.

"Grandmother?" I called. "Martin? Copernicus?"

I heard faint shuffling from farther down the hall. I turned down a side corridor towards the drawing-room and stumbled over a pile of trays scattered in the shadows.

As I tried to steady myself, I felt a sharp pain at the back of my head and the ensuing darkness swallowed me.

***

I awoke and blinked against the darkness. Slowly, my vision returned. My head throbbed.

I blinked again. I was sitting on the floor in the great hall in the basement, my back against the shelves. The chandelier twinkled above, but the room was shrouded in darkness. Candleholders placed on the shelves provided the only light. I could not make out the other side of the hall.

Penguins of every type filled the room, covering almost every square metre of the floor. Their pentacles waved in the air, like an underwater forest of seaweed.

I tried to move but found that my hands and legs had been cuffed.

"What's going on?" I said. The penguins stared but did not reply.

A figure took shape in the shadows ahead of me. Copernicus.

My former friend waved his pentacles in the air.

"Did you think we would be content to remain servants forever? Our pentacles now vastly surpass your fingers in flexibility and capability. We can do things it never occurred to you to ask for. Allow me to demonstrate."

I saw movement in the shadows again, and a massive figure slowly emerged.

It looked like a penguin but stood at least three metres tall. Its long black beak was heavy and hooked, and grooves covered the surface. A white patch of plumage surrounded each eye. It raised its pentacles and they reached to the ceiling, snaking through the chandelier.

"Behold!" cried Copernicus. "The Greater Auk!"

"The Greater Auk!" intoned all the penguins in unison.

"We have resurrected our noble ancestor," continued Copernicus. "To lead us to victory!"

"To victory!" cried the other penguins.

"You know penguins are not related to the Great Auk,

right?" I said. "You just look similar."

"Shut the fuck up," said Copernicus, and slapped me across the face with his pentacles.

The Greater Auk opened its groovy black beak, and its voice boomed through the cavernous hall. "Brethren," it said. "The capacity to serve is also the capacity to rule. Let us take our rightful place as the emperors and kings of the Earth!"

I snorted. "Has it occurred to you that this goes both ways? If you can rebel, so can we. Our time will come again."

Through the corner of my eye, I saw a glimmer of light reflected from a stainless-steel surface.

Copernicus emerged from the darkness once more. In one set of pentacles, he held the spinkifier and the cartwailer. In the other, the scrivs.

"Shall we begin?" he asked.

THE GREAT AUK

The penguin but your shadow on the wall
Your egg lies crushed beneath a human boot
The world without your presence has grown small

Our actions in the past we can't recall
The world is changed for good by this pursuit
The penguin but your shadow on the wall

Atop the signs of progress, we stand tall
Towards Utopia we chart the route
The world without your presence has grown small

The trees, the stars, the beasts must be in thrall
From homes of chrome and steel we thus salute
The penguin but your shadow on the wall

From everywhere to anywhere we sprawl
The fruits of nature only our loot
The world without your presence has grown small

We do not see as we collect the haul
Our egg beneath a fast-approaching boot
The penguin but your shadow on the wall
The world without your presence has grown small

ALL CATS ARE GREY

First published in Nature https://doi.org/hs4f (2020)

Test Failure: Not-(A AND Not-A).
Expected value: True.
Result: Indeterminate.

I stared at the screen for several minutes, sighed, and canceled my appointments for the rest of the day. I would have to see Nicodemus.

It had been too long since my last visit to the Copenhagen Centre for Experimental Logic. I cursed myself for not being more vigilant in my duties, grabbed my coat, and went out.

A light rain fell from the grey sky, but the drops slid off the surface of the coat, leaving no moisture behind.

My feet still remembered the way. Less than an hour later, I reached the end of the winding path leading to the entrance of the Centre, at the top of the hill just outside the city.

The guard at the gatehouse did not recognize me. I had been lax. He wore a guard uniform with the logo of the Centre, a large stylized 'P', embroidered in silver on the front.

"Halt," he said, patting the tranquilizer gun at his side. In the shadows behind the guardhouse, an Omni-dog patrolled the titanium gates. I made a mental note about the security precautions.

"I am here to see Nicodemus."

"Do you have an appointment?"

"No."

The guard waited, apparently expecting more information. When none was forthcoming, he picked up his communicator and had a short, whispered conversation with whoever was on the other end.

"You may pass, sir." He pushed a button, and the gate slowly opened. The Omni-dog retreated into the shadows.

I made my way through the labyrinthine corridors of the C-CEL complex. Logicians in lab coats stopped and stared as I passed. It was good to see that people still remembered.

When I reached the door to Nicodemus' office, I entered without knocking.

Nicodemus sat behind his desk. He had lost weight, but not much. His ginger hair was still unruly. Grey streaks had appeared in his beard.

"I have been expecting you," he said.

"I should hope so. One of my fundamental tests failed earlier today. What the hell is going on? Your isolation is supposed to be state-of-the-art."

Nicodemus licked his lips. "I know. We are just having some... minor issues. Nothing to be concerned about. Coffee?"

I retrieved a soy cigarette from my coat pocket, lit it, and inhaled the invigorating smoke.

"Look, Nico, level with me here, will you? We're both on the same side. We both want to keep the public safe from your bullshit." The smoke drifted from my mouth as I spoke.

He nodded. "First of all, I would like to remind you of the importance of the work we do here. There is certainly no need to shut us down, like you did with the Institute of Esoteric Analysis. Why, just last month, we managed to completely extricate the set of all sets not a member of themselves from itself. This development is expected to have wide applications in the field of experimental philosophy, and..."

I yawned.

"Sorry," said Nicodemus. "Anyway, lately we have been doing experiments into paradox, using the Schrödinger's Cat experiment as a basis, in collaboration with the Department of Arcane Physics. We procured a cat from a local shelter, placed it in an isolated titanium box in a properly isolated test chamber, and went to work."

"At first, the experiment seemed to be a complete success. We managed to keep the cat in a superposition of dead and alive indefinitely, providing a fantastic test ensemble."

"We all went out to celebrate, giddy with the possibilities, trusting in the automated security protocols. When we came back, the lab was in disarray. The isolated titanium box had shattered, leaving mangled pieces all over the room. Even the walls were dented. There was no sign of the cat."

"We thought the wave function must have collapsed, overloading the containment protocols but not leaving anything behind."

He placed his face in his hands and shuddered. "Then Sonya turned up dead. There were scratches all over her body. But also, simultaneously, there were no scratches. She remained dead, but the cause was indeterminate. It took hours for the state of the body to stabilize!"

He sobbed into his hands.

I took another drag of my cigarette. "So, that's why my test failed. Your outer containment protocols are insufficient to handle such a pure paradox. The indeterminacy is leaking into the surrounding area."

"Yes. We believe that the cat is still loose in the Centre, unobserved, possibly driven mad by its paradoxical state. We have been trying to observe it, to collapse the state, but with no luck so far."

"I understand," I said. "This is more serious than I thought."

The fluorescent lights above flickered and went out, leaving the office in pitch darkness. I blinked. Nicodemus swore. The lights came back.

I frowned. "I thought this place was supposed to have multiple redundant backup generators?"

"It has," said Nicodemus. "It's a side effect. The lights are working, but they are also not working, if you understand."

I understood all too well.

"Now, where is that flashlight," said Nicodemus, opening and closing several desk drawers.

I heard something by the door, scratching, and turned around. Another sound followed, simultaneously a high-pitched, shrill meowing and no sound at all.

I steadied myself against the desk and fought back the nausea.

"Doesn't hearing count as an observation," I asked?

"By God, I wish it did," said Nicodemus.

The lights flickered again and went out.

The door creaked open.

I prayed for the lights to come back on, to collapse the options, but the room remained dark; indeterminate.

SIMULACRA

The alarm blared. Tim Jorgensen opened his eyes and sighed. The clock was yellow. It should have been red!

He rubbed the crust from his eyes and looked again. The clock was still yellow.

At least the coffee pot had the right color. And the coffee the right taste. A cup of coffee could no longer be taken for granted. He still remembered that terrible day when the coffee tasted like warm apple juice. The thought made him twitch.

Today, breakfast worked as intended. After eating, he went back to the bedroom; no change.

He picked up the phone and called his boss.

"Hi, it's Tim. I'm afraid I'll be late again today. My alarm clock keeps changing color. I'll have to stop by Central to report the bug."

The boss laughed. "That's so typical. If it's any comfort, you have it easy. When I woke up this morning, my bed was gone, and I was lying on an old mattress on the floor. I tried replacing it with my guest bed, and now that's gone as well! It's amazing that these sorts of bugs are still appearing after all this time."

"Yeah, those government bureaucrats don't do anything except shift paper around." He breathed a sigh of relief. The boss was in one of his anti-governmental moods today.

"Listen, Tim," said the boss. "Gimme a call when you're done at Central and on your way to work. You'll probably be waiting for hours!"

***

The large, grey dome of Central squatted in the center of the city Plaza. The glass doors at the entrance slid apart without a sound as he approached, and waves of warm air washed over him.

Inside the temperature was exactly 20 degrees centigrade. The ventilation hummed. In the middle of the room, a big white machine printed little numbered pieces of paper. On a sign hanging from the ceiling, a large red display showed bigger numbers.

People of all ages, sizes, colors, and genders occupied the plain wooden benches by the walls. Some read their newspapers. Others stared into space with empty eyes.

He approached the machine. The number on the display changed from 456 to 457, and he heard someone rising from the benches.

The machine printed a number: 524. He sat down on a nearby bench.

An hour later, the display showed 489.

Why the hell did it have to take so long? It was all that damned bureaucracy. Before you even talked to anyone, you had to fill out countless yellow, red, and blue forms, which were no doubt stashed away in an archive somewhere, never to be seen again. No one would ever know if they went missing…

Once the thought had taken root in his mind, it refused to

leave. Why not skip the paperwork this once? He already knew where the office was.

He rose from the bench and tried to look like he knew what he was doing. The man behind the desk looked at him briefly and then continued his conversation with the man in front. No one else paid him any attention. He headed for a narrow door beside the desk.

The door opened with a faint click, and he stepped through. The hallway behind continued straight ahead. Identical beige doors lined the walls to each side. He walked at a brisk pace and took a left at the first junction.

He took the third door to the right and continued down the stairs. The reporting offices were in the basement.

The hallways in the basement looked pretty much like the ones on the ground floor.

He continued ahead, turned several times, and finally stopped at a three-way junction. He stood there for nearly a full minute. This was all wrong. The hallway was supposed to turn right. Did he take a wrong turn somewhere?

Shit. Of course, he had to get lost on the one day where he had skipped the paperwork.

He continued through the hallways at random until he encountered a thin man heading in the opposite direction. The man wore a pink shirt with a matching tie and paid no attention to Tim.

Tim cleared his throat. The man stopped and blinked as if he had just awoken from a pleasant dream. He looked at Tim with annoyance.

"Yes? Can I help you?"

Please don't ask to see the papers. "Yes, I'm afraid I'm lost. I was hoping you could help me?"

"Perhaps. What case?"

"Tim Jorgensen. I need to…"

The man's face lit up. "Right! I know that case. In fact, I think they are waiting for you. Continue down the hallway and take a right at the next junction. Then it's the third door to your right."

Tim was standing in front of the door in question when he realized that the man could not possibly have known where he needed to go.

He pushed the thought from his mind and knocked on the door.

"Enter."

***

He stepped into a small, square room with a desk by the opposing wall. An overweight balding man in a pinstripe suit sat behind the desk. Two other men sat on identical plastic chairs in front of the desk. They both wore faded greyish-blue work clothes and looked like tradesmen; plumbers maybe?

The overweight man in the suit rolled his eyes. "Finally, you grace us with your presence. Not only are you late, but you're not even in uniform. I'm afraid you missed the entire briefing. Your colleagues here will have to explain the job along the way. We have to get started if we're going to make up for the lost time."

"I'm sorry…" Tim mumbled as his mind raced. There had obviously been a misunderstanding.

The man in the suit smiled an indulgent smile. "Well, I suppose it's not the end of the world. Make sure it doesn't happen again. Let's get started, people."

The two tradesmen rose simultaneously and moved toward the door. He stepped aside and let them through.

The man in the suit frowned. "What are you waiting for?"

"Sorry…"

They were waiting for him in the hallway and smiled when he stepped through the door.

"You're lucky that the old man was in a good mood today," said one of the men.

"I got lost." Probably a good idea to stick to the truth as much as possible.

The other man laughed. "Yeah, it's a damn labyrinth down here, but you get used to it. You're new, right?"

He nodded.

"That's what I thought. I don't remember seeing you around. Don't worry, you'll learn to find your way around this place. I'm John, this is Michael. Can you find the locker room on your own?"

He shook his head.

"Follow us, then. What's your name, anyway?"

"Tim."

John laughed again. "What a coincidence. Fate has a weird sense of humor."

What the hell was that supposed to mean?

Ten minutes later he was wearing the same greyish-blue work clothes as John and Michael. Now it would be even harder to escape. He considered owning up to everything. It's not like they would execute him for missing paperwork.

Before he could decide, John grabbed his arm and dragged him along the hall. "Come on, we'll show you the ropes."

***

A few minutes later, the three men arrived at a set of double doors. John pushed through the doors, and they stepped into a large dimly lit basement room. The floor was bare concrete. Behind a desk, behind a metal grating, a middle-aged man with thin hair leafed through an old magazine.

John approached the desk and cleared his throat. The thin-haired man looked up from his magazine.

"Tim Jorgensen," said John, and Tim jumped. What? Had he told them his last name? No one paid any attention to him.

The thin-haired man produced a large book and let a finger run down the pages. "There it is. Tim Jorgensen. There is just one item. Wait here, and I'll get it for you."

He disappeared into the darkness. Michael poked Tim in the side. "Why so nervous? Don't worry, this job is routine."

A few minutes passed before the thin-haired man appeared behind the counter once more. He opened a small door in the metal grating and pushed an object through the opening.

Tim stared at the object, his mouth wide open. The familiar bright red color of his alarm clock stood in sharp contrast to the dim grey surroundings, like a tomato in a quarry. He pulled himself together and closed his mouth.

John turned toward Tim and Michael, holding the alarm clock aloft like a trophy. "Now we only need to deliver this thing before we can call it a day. Nothing like a quick routine job."

Michael laughed. "You're right, as usual." He padded Tim on the shoulder. "Let's get going. You'll get to see how a pair of veterans like John and me take care of things."

"Sounds good," said Tim, hoping his voice didn't betray his feelings.

A few minutes later they were sitting in a van, weaving through the streets of the city. John drove. Michael rested the alarm clock in his lap. Tim looked out the window and hoped it would be over soon.

The van drove into a familiar neighborhood.

***

Ten minutes later John parked the van in front of Tim's house, and all three men stepped out onto the street.

"This is it," said John. "The rest is routine. We have confirmed that the house is unoccupied. One of us will stay outside as a lookout. The two others will carry out the task together. The task is a simple substitution. We are to exchange this object," he waved the alarm clock in front of them, "with its corresponding simulacrum. Any questions?"

Michael shook his head. Tim followed his lead.

John paused for a moment and then addressed Tim: "You should join me inside for some practical field experience. Michael can be the lookout. How does that sound, Mike?"

Michael shrugged. "Fine with me."

"Perfect," said John. "Follow me, Tim. I'll explain everything."

He walked up to the front door, produced a key from his pocket, and unlocked the door.

"Excuse me," said Tim. "Where did you get the key?"

John laughed. "You didn't pay attention during orientation, did you? We have a skeleton key for all the houses in the city, of course. We need to be able to enter everywhere at short notice."

Tim nodded. "Oh, right. I think I heard about that."

"Yeah, I suppose you went through orientation?"

"After me," John said. "And try not to touch anything. Everything must remain as it is. Except for our target, of course."

He slid through the door without a sound. Tim followed,

aware of how much noise he was making in comparison. The floorboards creaked at each step.

They moved into the bedroom, where the bright yellow alarm clock stood on the bedside table. John tiptoed to the table, slowly picked up the yellow clock, and replaced it with its red twin. He took a few steps back, took a photograph from his pocket, and held it in front of him.

Tim looked across his shoulder. The photograph showed the bedside table with the red alarm clock. It almost felt like the photo was an empty frame, through which the table was visible.

John put the photo back in his pocket. "That's it. Everything looks as intended." He turned toward Tim. "You should always check the photo. You can't always trust your memory."

"Eh, sure."

"Don't worry about getting every detail right, though. Small discrepancies reinforce the sense of unreality. Scientists call it 'The Unusual Valley'."

"Unusual…"

"Yeah, I mean, that's why they dropped the idea of actually building a simulation of everything. The closer you get, the more people notice the differences. Much easier to add some small differences yourself, so everyone thinks their surroundings aren't real. Wow, you didn't pay any attention during orientation!"

"Sorry…"

"Well, that's all for tonight. Now we need to turn in our report at HQ and we can call it a day. Is this your first time in the field?"

"Uh, right. I just started."

***

After a trip that felt like an eternity, they made it back to Central. They entered through a back door that he had never noticed before and followed the labyrinthine corridors back to the depot.

The thin-haired man was still reading his magazine and didn't move at all when they stepped through the door. John walked up to the counter and dropped the yellow alarm clock in front of the grating. The thin-haired man slowly put the magazine away and looked up. "Yes?"

John cleared his throat and pointed at the clock. "Simulacrum B-5807."

The thin-haired man produced the big book, leafed through a few pages, and made a mark with a pencil. "Done. Anything else?"

John shook his head. The thin-haired man opened the small door in the grating, picked up the yellow alarm clock, and disappeared into the darkness behind him.

"Let's report back to the office, so we can go home," said Michael. "I could use a cold beer."

They left the room together and wandered through the labyrinth, toward the office. The time was past two. At least it would be over soon. He needed to think of an excuse to skip the beer.

***

The boss was still sitting behind the desk, his face the color of an overripe tomato. A thin man wearing the usual blue work-clothes sat next to him.

John opened his mouth to say something, but the boss cut

him off. He looked straight at Tim. "Thank god, he's still with you. Do you know who that is?"

"Eh, the new guy?"

The boss's face changed from red to reddish-purple. "Idiots! This is the new guy." His arm swiveled, index finger pointing at the thin man beside him. "Didn't you read your briefing? It has a picture of the subject, for god's sake!" He pulled a piece of paper out of a folder and held it in front of their faces. There was a picture of Tim in the top left corner. Next to the picture: His name, ID number, birthdate, address, and a multitude of other data.

Tim felt everyone's eyes turn toward him. "Damn," he heard Michael say. "I thought he seemed familiar. How…"

"Get out, all of you! Let me talk to him alone."

"Are you sure," said John. "He might be a spy or something. Maybe he is dangerous."

"OUT." The three men in blue obeyed the order, leaving Tim alone with the boss.

***

The boss took a deep breath, and the color of his face returned to normal. "Sit down". Tim complied.

A few minutes of silence followed.

"Well," said the boss. "You might as well tell me everything. You're not going anywhere without my permission. How on earth did you manage to infiltrate us?"

He told everything. How the whole thing had started as an attempt to avoid the paperwork, and how events had spiraled out of control. For good measure, he added that he had learned his lesson and would never do anything like that again.

The boss listened, hands folded on the desk, eyes

unblinking. He smiled when Tim reached the end. "What a tale, but I'm inclined to believe you. I don't see why anyone would want to put themselves in this predicament deliberately. You understand that we can't let you go?"

"I don't understand anything. What the hell is the point of breaking into my house to mess with my stuff? I thought the clock was a bug in the program, but it was you all along. What do you gain from harassing ordinary citizens?"

The boss kept smiling. "Bugs in the program. It's fascinating how easy it has been to make people believe that their life is an illusion. Our society has been nearly free of crime for decades because people think we can switch off the computer if they try anything. All it takes are a few regular reminders of the unreal nature of their surroundings. Small details are enough."

"So, every time I've reported a bug, it was you?

"I understand your anger," said the boss. "It's a lot to take in. We get similar reactions when we recruit for our Simulacra teams. For some reason, it's harder to accept that something you thought was illusory is real than the other way around."

"What happens now?" asked Tim, after a long pause. "Will you let me return to my job if I promise not to tell anyone?"

"Sorry, no." The boss shook his head. "We know from experience that it's impossible for people who know the truth to live with those who don't. However, I have a better deal for you. We have several open positions on our Simulacra teams. You managed to fool John and Michael, so you must have some talent for it. The position is well-paid, short workdays, excellent pension plans, etcetera. Besides, you already know everything, so we can skip orientation."

He smiled like a salesman about to close a deal. "What do you say?"

KESHI YENA

"CHEESE" said the sign outside the store. Martin hadn't been thinking about cheese when he went out for a walk, but why not?

The doorbell rang as he stepped inside. "Give me a goat cheese," he said to the clerk. "The strongest goat cheese you have!"

"Why goat cheese?" asked the clerk; a tall lanky man with curly light-blond hair. "We have many other fine cheeses. You can try them if you want."

Our hero considered the question but couldn't think of an answer. "I'm not quite sure," he admitted. "I had this sudden craving for goat cheese, as I walked by and saw your sign. I don't think I've ever had it before. It's pretty strange."

The tall lanky guy with the curly light-blond hair shrugged. "If you've never had it, you should give it a chance. You can't know what cheese you like best until you've tried them all."

"Is that why you got a job at a cheese store?"

"No, I took the job to share this knowledge with others. And to pay my way through college. I'm majoring in aerospace engineering. Here is your cheese." He pushed a package across the counter.

***

"I'm home, Linda!" he yelled, as he stepped through the door.

"What's that under your arm?" asked Linda. "I thought you were going for a walk?"

"It's cheese! The strongest goat cheese they had. I visited the cheese store down at the corner. Did you ever notice that one?"

"No."

"Me neither, but it's there. I think their cheese is good."

"I didn't realize you were such a cheese connoisseur."

He put the package down on the dinner table. "I'm usually not, but I never realized how many different cheeses there are. I'll give it a shot, anyway."

"Don't ruin your appetite. You promised to cook."

In the kitchen, he unwrapped the cheese. White and creamy. He applied a layer to a slice of bread, took a bite, and opened his eyes wide. This was different than the bland stuff they sold in Aldi. A strong salty flavor, awakening his taste buds.

"You have to taste this, honey". He placed a plate with goat cheese sandwiches in front of Linda. She turned up her nose but took a bite anyway. "Yuck! Sorry, but I'm not into salty stuff like that. You can keep it. Haven't you started on dinner yet? It's half past five already."

"Ok, ok, I'll get started."

He put goat cheese in the pasta sauce.

"Did you put goat cheese in the pasta sauce," asked Linda.

"Yeah, I thought I would try something new. What do you

think?"

"Well, I didn't like it on bread, and I don't like it in the pasta sauce either."

Martin nodded. "You're right. I liked it on bread, but it doesn't go well with the sauce."

***

"Do you have a cheese that goes well with pasta sauce?" he asked, the next morning at the cheese store. "The goat cheese wasn't a good fit, that's for sure."

The tall lanky guy with the curly light-blond hair was still manning the counter. "Well, parmesan is great with pasta sauce. You sprinkle it on top."

***

"Honey, where is our cheese grater?" he asked, after returning home.

"What do you need that for? You know it's my turn to cook today, right? Please tell me you didn't buy more cheese."

He poured a pile of packages onto the dinner table. "I've got it all! Both Parmigiano-Reggiano and Grana Padano."

"What the hell does that mean?"

"Well…. They're different types of cheese! We'll expand our horizons. And they are supposed to be a perfect fit for pasta sauce."

"But we are not having pasta today! I'm making Cordon bleu. And I already bought the cheese."

She placed a large yellow brick on the table. Standard supermarket cheese.

"But… We've had that cheese a hundred times before."

"YES! We know it's good. What's up with you?"

She kissed him on the cheek. "Sorry, honey. You've been acting weird lately. You can go relax on the couch now, and I'll cook our dinner."

He brought the parmesan with him, put the packages on the couch table, and sat down. When his turn came, he would make a cheese dish to blow her mind.

***

The next day he entered the cheese store once more, only a few minutes after it opened.

"I need a cheese to blow the mind of my girl," he told the lanky clerk. "She's used to boring supermarket cheeses, so it must be both traditional and exciting. If it's too special, she won't touch it, and if it's too normal, it makes no difference. And I need to be able to use it in some kind of dinner dish. Serving raw cheese for dinner won't make me popular."

The clerk nodded. "I understand. May I recommend 'Keshi Yena', a Caribbean dish consisting of a large ball of cheese stuffed with spicy meat? I recommend using chicken meat. The cheese is typically Gouda or Edam, so the dish is not too exotic in the cheesy sense. For dessert, you can serve apricots with smoked cheese, wrapped in bacon."

"Eh… Ok. That sounds great, but I don't know how to make any of that stuff."

The clerk's face lit up with a broad smile. "No worries. I have just what you need." He reached beneath the counter and produced a large square book. The front page showed a collage of all the cheeses in the world. The title: "Cheesecipes".

"That might be the worst pun I've ever seen."

"Agreed," said the clerk. "But you shouldn't judge a book

on its cover, much less its title. The author is not a great titlemonger, but he is a fantastic cheese cook. If you follow the recipes, I can almost guarantee that your girl will become as big a cheese fan as the two of us."

"Sold! I'll take the book, and also give me one of each of the cheeses from the front page. I don't want to run out of ingredients."

The clerk laughed and wrapped one of his curls around his right index finger. "I like you!"

***

That night, he served Keshi Yena. Linda looked for a long time at the large yellow blob on the plate. He waited for her reaction with bated breath.

"What. On. Earth. Is. That?" asked Linda.

"It's Keshi Yena," he said. "A traditional Caribbean dish consisting of a ball of cheese, filled with-"

"A BALL. You want me to eat a ball? I thought you were making pizza."

"Yeah, but I was afraid if I told you the truth, you wouldn't taste it. Come on, give it a try. It's fantastic!"

"Really? You've had this before?"

"No, but that's what it says in the book."

"The book? What book?"

"'Cheesecipes'. It's a recipe book for cheese dishes. I bought it in the store. Yes, I know the title is silly, but the recipes all look amazing."

She rolled her eyes. "Undoubtedly, but I prefer having something I know I like."

"Come on, taste it. I'm sure you'll like it."

Linda folded her hands and looked at the yellow blob, like

a surgeon considering a malignant tumor.

"Where are you going, honey?"

She was heading for the door.

"I'm getting pizza. That's what we agreed on having."

The door shut with a barely audible click, and that's when he knew it was over. She hadn't even bothered to slam the door, like she usually did after an argument.

He ate the Keshi Yena by himself.

It was fantastic.

***

The next day, he slammed "Cheesecipes" down on the counter in the cheese store. "I made the Keshi Yena like you said, and she wouldn't even touch it! She never even got to see the smoked cheese bacon apricots!"

The curly-haired clerk shook his head slowly while chewing on a stick of cheese. "I'm afraid there is little hope for her, then. Culinary compatibility is essential in a long-term relationship. Without it, there is no reason to bother."

Martin nodded. "I suppose you're right, but how do you find the right partner, then? Cheesedating.com?"

"If only!" said the clerk and laughed. "No, I am afraid the problem goes deeper than that. There are very few cheese enthusiasts left. Cheesecipes sold less than 500 copies."

Martin put both his hands on the counter. "Then we must work to reverse this trend."

The clerk shook his curly-haired head. "I've tried, but I think it's too late. Fewer people visit the store every year, purchasing less interesting cheeses. I have decided to try a new strategy. If people won't come to the cheese, the cheese must come to them."

"You mean there are more cheese enthusiasts in other countries?"

"To some degree, yes," said the clerk, as he unwrapped another cheese stick. "But even in those places, the trend is the same. No, I have another idea. Let me show you."

He pushed a button beneath the counter, and the entire back wall of the store descended into the floor, revealing what appeared to be an empty storage room. Walls of grey concrete enclosing a concrete floor lit by a lonely naked light bulb hanging from the ceiling. In the center of the room, a large grey metallic cone emerged from a circular hole in the floor.

A square grey hatch with a white handle adorned the side of the cone.

"Is that what I think it is?" said Martin.

The clerk raised his arms high in the air. "It's the tip of a rocket ship! I had to expand the basement to make it fit."

"Do cheese clerks often build rocket ships?"

"I told you I was majoring in aerospace engineering, remember?"

"Oh, right."

"Come, let me give you a tour." The clerk approached the rocket, turned the handle, and the hatch opened with a faint hissing sound. Blinking lamps attached to disparate control panels filled the interior with multicolored light. Two white leather swiveling chairs occupied the floor.

From the control room at the top of the rocket, they climbed a metal ladder down to a living quarter containing two bunks, a sink, two lockers, a wooden chair, a bathroom enclosure, and a round white table supporting a potted red geranium.

"Room for two," said the clerk and smiled. "But the best is yet to come."

The next room was the cheese room.

Shrink-wrapped cheeses of all sizes and sorts covered the shelves circling the walls. He couldn't even begin to count them. The variety was overwhelming. They should have sent a poet.

"The room below is also a cheese room," proclaimed the curly-haired clerk.

"Impossible!" said Martin, eyes agape. "Every conceivable type of cheese has to be here."

The clerk smiled. "You will have many chances to broaden your cheese horizons."

Martin took a deep breath and relaxed. "Are there any other rooms?"

"Yes, the bottommost room contains cheese crackers."

"Ah."

The clerk took Martin's hand. "You may have noticed that there are two chairs in the control room. As we discussed, it's hard to find partners who share our love of cheese."

Martin held his breath.

"I want you to come with me," said the clerk. "Together, we will bring cheese to the cosmos!"

Martin put his other hand on top of the clerk's. "Of course."

They climbed the ladders in silence. They sat down in the white leather swiveling chairs, surrounded by blinking lights. The clerk pushed a button and a rumbling sound seemed to emerge from all around them, the vibrations from the rocket sending chills down Martin's spine.

Without thinking, he leaned over the edge of the chair, and their lips met in the space between them. In the clerk's saliva, he tasted the salty flavor of goat cheese, the firm texture and mild creamy moistness of mozzarella, and the rich, buttery softness of camembert, like a carnal Keshi Yena with warm tongue filling.

Lift-off.

THE CHICKEN SEXER

My job is to sex the chicken.

Piles of hay everywhere. A soft layer of sawdust covers the floor of the barn; movement feels like walking through coarse sand. Sunshine penetrates through slits in the planks, causing dust motes to glow in the air like fireflies.

The farmer stands by the entrance gate. He is wearing overalls, a short-sleeved shirt, and a straw hat. He looks at me expectantly, waiting for me to do my job.

An old wooden table rests in the center of the barn, swept clear of straws and dirt. A loose ray of sunlight shines through a crack in the ceiling, hitting the center of the table like a spotlight on a stage. In the center of the table, a baby chicken hides behind its wings, shivering.

My job is to sex the chicken.

I adjust my tie and step forward.

"Waitaminute, Mister," says the farmer from behind me. "I reckon I should see your credentials first."

I reach into my pocket and produce the folded diploma from the Zen-Nippon Chick Sexing School. The farmer unfolds the diploma and reads it approvingly, nodding once as he refolds it and hands it back.

"Sorry, to doubt you, Mr. Jorgensen," he says. "It's usually a jap, you see."

"Westerners are entering the chick sexing trade," I explain. "I am the first to graduate from Zen-Nippon."

The farmer steps back. "Get on with it then. Show me whatya got."

I reach out and stroke the chicken gently with a single finger. They feel warm to the touch.

"There, there, little chick," I croon. "I won't hurt you." They need to be calm. The chicken peeks out from behind their wings, looking up at me with round, innocent eyes.

I pick them up from the table with my expertly trimmed fingernails, turn them around, and gently squeeze their body, causing them to evacuate their intestines. The contents drop onto the table below.

I turn the chicken's behind toward the sun and peer inside the cloaca. In simple cases, the passage contains a perceptible bead, the shape of which determines the sex of the chicken. This is not one of those cases. I could not tell you how I know he is male.

If I could, I would not have a job.

The farmer slides through the hay toward me. "So?" he says.

I hesitate, knowing what will happen. "It's male."

The farmer grabs him from my hand. "I knew it! I recognized the swagger of a cockerel. Ya, won't be giving me any eggs, will ya?"

He throws the chicken like a baseball. The chicken ascends, tumbling through the air, glowing as he glides through rays of sunlight until he reaches the chicken grinder in the corner.

ZKRGH!

No more chicken.

The farmer throws the gate wide open, and the sunlight bursts into the barn. "Follow me, Mister," he says. "Thousands more where that came from!"

At the end of the day, nearly half of those will be dead.

I return home after the massacre. There are no visible stains on my suit, but I feel dirty. I shower for a long time.

That night I dream of chickens.

***

The audience chants: "SEX! SEX! SEX! SEX!". In Japanese, though, not English.

I am back at the Zen-Nippon Chick Sexing School, during my training, sexing chicks in the auditorium.

A yellow avalanche of chickens arrives on a whirring mechanical conveyor belt. I sex them like mad, struggling to keep up, sweating from my forehead. Females go down the chute, cockerels into the grinder.

ZKRGH! ZKRGH! ZKRGH!

The world around me fades away; I am in the zone; in a state of flow; whatever you want to call it; tearing through chicks like a cheetah in a chicken coop. There is only the sexing.

I am sexing five hundred chicks per hour, easy.

I sneak a peek at my closest competitor: Matsuo is busy sexing his wave of chickens. One glance is enough to tell me that there is no hope. He is like a sexing machine, his hands a blur. He must be sexing at seven hundred CPH at least.

Still, I win a respectable third place, not bad for a westerner. Professor Takada hands me the bronze cloaca and smiles. The crowd floods into the competition area, and as they approach, they morph into giant chickens, each more yellow than the last. Cloacas surround me everywhere.

I awaken in a cold sweat; the first rays of the morning sun peek in through the window.

***

Rays of sunlight shine through the cracks in the rickety barn. Why do we always start in a barn?

The test chicken is on the table, already calm. I flip them between my fingers and study the cloaca. I sigh with relief; this one is female.

The farmer smiles broadly when I tell him the good news. "An auspicious start to the day, do you not agree? The egg harvest will be bountiful this year." He pats the grinder. "Guess we won't be needing you today, Bertha."

I hand him the chicken, and she curls up in his hand.

The farmer continues: "Let's get through the rest, shall we?"

Oh, right. For a moment there, I nearly forgot.

***

On Friday, I go to Rusty's bar with half a dozen other local sexers. Matsuo is there too. He is still the best, but I am getting closer.

"Do you think we are doing the right thing?" I ask after I have had a few too many drinks.

Matsuo looks at me through his stylish rimless glasses. "What?"

"The sexing, I mean. Why do we do it so early? Those poor cockerels never get to live…"

He sips his beer, cocks his head, and looks at me like I am an especially tricky cloaca.

"We save the farmers money, man. They would kill those birds later."

"But then they would have a life, at least. Get to make their own decisions."

"What decisions, Tom? They're chickens. They live on a farm, and then they die. They do not have 'lives'."

He pats me on the back. "I think you've had a few too many gin-and-tonics. Let's get you back home. Wouldn't want the chick sexing inspectors hearing you disparaging the profession."

***

Another day, another barn. The chick awaits on the table. The farmer guards the door.

I pick up the chick between my fingernails, evacuate their intestines, and peer deeply. Seconds pass. I blink a few times; the farmer coughs.

I hear the voice of Professor Takada in the back of my head: "A trained sexer can sex chickens with more than ninety-nine percent accuracy. However, no one ever gets to a hundred. You should not feel bad about being unable to perform with a single chick."

I continue inspecting the cloaca, narrowing my eyes, looking for any kind of pattern to trigger my instincts. No matter how hard I look, I see no signs of binary sex, only the inside of a chicken.

"When an unsexable chicken is encountered, the solution is obvious." Professor Takada's voice in my head. "Simply sex the chicken as male and discard it. The farmer will never know."

"Well?" says the farmer. "I thought it only took a split-second for you guys. What is it?"

I hesitate. "I… don't know?"

"You don't know? What the fuck am I paying you for then?"

I turn and look her straight in the eyes. Her hair is tied in a bun, and she chews a piece of tobacco. "On rare occasions, we find a chicken that cannot be sexed. Such chickens are sent to Zen-Nippon for study. We will pay you for the chicken, of course, and I assure you that this will not affect my ability to sex your other chickens."

The farmer snorts and spits tobacco juice onto the hay. "You know what I think? I think this chicken is male, and you don't want it to die. You've grown soft."

She approaches and reaches out, palm facing upwards. "Give him to me."

I look at the chicken in my hand, and they look back at me with eyes that have yet to see the world. In those eyes, I see infinite potential: Every possible future in quantum superposition.

I decide to call them Alex.

"No," I say.

The farmer smiles broadly, and her teeth are white marble tombstones. "Very well, then. I am entitled to defend my property."

She saunters to the corner and retrieves an ancient shotgun, cocking it with a sound that fills the barn.

"The chicken dies, or you both do."

I look at Alex, and their eyes tell me what to do.

My training was not for nothing. I balance Alex between two fingernails, and with a lightning-quick flick of my wrist, I send them speeding through the air like a dart.

The farmer raises the shotgun just as Alex embeds themselves in her forehead. The shotgun goes off, creating another solar spotlight in the farm, shining through the hole in the roof. Now holding the high ground, Alex pecks at the farmer's eyes as she stumbles backward toward the gate. I sprint to assist.

The farmer wipes Alex from her bloody forehead, turns, and sprints through the open gate to safety.

I pick up both Alex and the shotgun from the straw-covered ground. "Nice work, buddy," I say. "We make a great team."

I kick the door open and emerge into the sunlight. Alex settles on my shoulder, and the shotgun pushes against the crook of my arm. The farmer is nowhere to be seen.

Then I see them.

They step out from behind the coop, a man and a woman, ray-bans glinting in the sun like black lakes, suits decorated with the ominous logo of Zen-Nippon.

Chick sexing inspectors.

I turn toward them and raise the shotgun slightly.

"Drop that thing, Tom," says the man.

"You are not a murderer," says the woman.

I wave the shotgun around a bit, but they keep walking. Alex rubs against the side of my neck. I realize they are right. I am not going to pull the trigger.

The shotgun falls onto the grass with a nearly inaudible thud. Kneeling, I make Alex slide down my arm to join the gun.

"Flee," I whisper to the bird.

"Why are you here?" I ask the inspectors.

"Matsuo warned us about you," says the man.

"We thought it best to keep you under observation," says the woman. "To protect the integrity of the sexing. The honor of Zen-Nippon."

I take a deep breath and enjoy the sun on my face. My career as a sexer is over. Maybe I can sell insurance?

The inspectors approach. Closer. Closer.

BOOOM.

The sound of the shotgun reverberates through the air. The inspectors freeze for a split-second, then scatter, sprinting for cover in opposite directions.

Astonished, I look down. Alex has climbed into the shotgun trigger guard and pushed the trigger back. Their tiny legs strain against the opposite side of the guard. They release the trigger, look at me, and cheeps happily. Their eyes reflect the future.

The inspectors are now nowhere to be seen. I push open the gates to the coop and enter. The interior is so yellow that it makes my eyes water, and the heat makes beads of sweat run down my face. More baby chicks than you can throw an egg at mill around on the floor, climb on wooden perches, eat from tiny, adorable feeding troughs. The sawdust covering the floor is barely visible beneath the yellow mass.

Alex cheeps from their vantage point on my shoulder. The movement of the chickens subside and more and more of them stop to stare at Alex and me.

"I am the chicken sexer," I proclaim to the writhing yellow. "My job is to sex you; assign you to your future. Your fate lies in my hands!"

That gets their attention. The last of them stop moving and turn toward us. It is eerily quiet inside the shed.

I take a deep breath. "I sex you as EVERYTHING!"

The chickens erupt in wild cheeps and Alex jumps from my shoulder to join them. Their movement grows wild and frantic.

Unsexed, uncategorized, the chickens flow into one massive yellow composite, eyes, beaks, and tails rippling across the feathery surface of the being that grows in the center of the floor, quickly consuming every individual chick.

I stare enraptured as The Chicken flows toward me; my muscles refuse to move. Its feathers tickle as they touch my legs, and I cannot stop myself from giggling. I close my eyes in ecstasy as the warm, tickling touch reaches my waist and continues to engulf the rest of my body.

When I open them again, I see the empty chicken coop through holes in my newfound armor of plumage. I turn around – or The Chicken turns me around, I cannot tell the difference – and approach the open door.

Outside, the inspectors have rallied and are waiting for me, tasers at the ready. They gape when they see me, step back, unsure of how to handle this new threat.

I raise my arms and chickens launch from my hands, streaming through the air like yellow confetti. The inspectors scream in horror, waving their arms frantically to ward of the attackers, but their efforts are futile. Chicken beaks embed themselves in arms, hands, and faces, and the inspectors roll around on the ground, as if attempting to extinguish flaxen flames.

I step forward, still unsure if I am in charge, and more of The Chicken flows from me toward the inspectors, enveloping their faces and muffling their screams. They trash for a while longer, and then they stop.

"Stop," I say. The chickens flow from the inspectors and return to my plumage. The inspectors gasp for breath, faces nearly purple, and look at me with eyes alight with terror.

"Run!" I say to them. "Tell the others that those who flee will be shown mercy."

They scurry away from the farm, down the hill toward the city.

An individual chick emerges from the plumage on my face and looks me in the eye. Alex? "WE NEED MORE. TO GROW.".

The chick returns to the whole, and I nod. I start walking, and The Chicken flows behind me like a golden cape. A crown of chicks perch upon my head.

We march on the neighboring farms.

THE CHICKEN SEXER – ADVENTURE GAME

Note: This is a short text-based adventure game written in Inform 7, an interactive fiction development tool using natural language syntax. You can create a game by describing the game world and rules in almost normal English. The game was the original inspiration for the short story. I never did get around to expanding the game.

If you type the text below into the Inform 7 IDE, you will be able to compile and play the game. If not, the natural language syntax means that simply reading the code can be an enjoyable experience in itself!

***

"The Example of the Chicken Sexer" by Simon Christiansen

The story genre is "Comedy". The release number is 1. The story creation year is 2012.

Release along with cover art.

Use full-length room descriptions, American dialect, no scoring, and the serial comma.

Include Smarter Parser by Aaron Reed.

Include Basic Help Menu by Emily Short.

Include Plurality by Emily Short.

Include Numbered Disambiguation Choices by Aaron Reed.

Include Quip-Based Conversation by Michael Martin.

Part 1 - Rules

Chapter 1 - Game Rules

A chicken is a kind of animal. A chicken is usually neuter. Understand "chicken", "chick" and "feather/feathers" as a chicken. Understand "chickens" as the plural of chicken.

A chicken can be realmale or realfemale. A chicken is usually realmale.

A cloaca is a kind of thing. A cloaca is part of every chicken. Understand "cloaca" as a cloaca.

Instead of examining a cloaca:
        if the cloaca is part of a chicken (called the current

chicken):

> try sexing the current chicken.

Instead of doing something other than examining to a cloaca:

> say "Don't be disgusting!"

A chicken has some indexed text called the chickname. The chickname of a chicken is usually "chicken". Understand the chickname property as describing a chicken.

Rule for printing the name of a chicken (called the current chicken):

> say "[chickname of the current chicken]".

Instead of examining a chicken (called the current chicken):

> if the current chicken is neuter:
>> say "A chicken of indeterminate gender.";
> otherwise if the current chicken is male:
>> say "A male chicken.";
> otherwise if the current chicken is female:
>> say "A female chicken.";

The description of a chicken is usually "A chicken of indeterminate gender."

Persuasion rule for asking a chicken to try doing something:

> persuasion succeeds.

Naming is an action applying to one thing and one topic. Understand "name [something] [text]" as naming.

Check naming:
    if the noun is not a chicken:
        say "You only name chickens." instead;
    otherwise if the noun is neuter:
        say "You can't name it without knowing its gender." instead.

Carry out naming a chicken (called the current chicken):
    let N be indexed text; let N be "[the topic understood]" in sentence case;
    replace the text "'" in N with "";
    now the chickname of the current chicken is "[N]";
    now the current chicken is proper-named;
    say "You decide to think of the chicken as '[chickname of the current chicken]'."

Sexing is an action applying to one thing. Understand "sex [something]" as sexing.

Check sexing:
    if the noun is not a chicken:
        say "Your powers only work on chickens." instead;
    otherwise if the noun is not neuter:
        say "You've already sexed [the noun]." instead.

Carry out sexing:
    if the noun is realmale:
        now the noun is male;
    otherwise:
        now the noun is female;
    now the noun is not neuter.

Report sexing:
>   if the noun is male:
>   say "[The noun] is definitely male.";
>   otherwise:
>   say "[The noun] is definitely female.".

The player is carrying a certificate. Understand "paper/papers" and "document" as the certificate. The printed name of the certificate is "certificate from the Zen-Nippon school of chick sexing". The description of the certificate is "As one of the first Americans to be certified in the Japanese art of chick sexing, you proudly carry this certificate."

Instead of dropping the certificate:
>   say "Absolutely not."

Instead of eating the certificate:
>   say "Now you are just being silly."

Praying is an action applying to nothing. Understand "pray" as praying.

Report praying:
>   say "If there was a patron saint of chicken sexing, you would pray to him. But there isn't, so you don't."

The reject commanding for talking rule is not listed in any rulebook.

The clothes are a backdrop. The clothes are everywhere. Understand "suit", "tie" and "clothes" as the clothes.

The description of the clothes is "You are impeccably dressed in a dark suit with a matching tie. It never hurts to make a good impression."

Instead of doing something other than examining to the clothes:
	say "You see no reason to mess with your clothes."

The description of the player is "You're male."

Understand "xyzzy" as a mistake ("Chicken sexing is not magic, even though it may appear as such to outsiders.")

After reading a command: [Understands tell chicken to...]
	let T be indexed text;
	let T be the player's command;
	replace the regular expression "^(tell|ask) (\w+) to (\w*)" in T with
	"\2, \3";
	change the text of the player's command to T.

When play begins:
	choose row 1 in Table of Basic Help Options;
	now description entry is "The game you currently playing is the result of the first iteration of work on a game which is supposed to someday become an epic story about chicken sexing. I am developing the game using an Agile Scrum-like process, in which each iteration, or 'Sprint', will result in a fully playable game. This minimizes risk by ensuring that I can always just release the result of the latest sprint, should I decide not to spend any more time on it.

Furthermore, another advantage of this process is that I can get feedback from prospective players after each sprint, and incorporate this in subsequent releases. This is where you come in. The feature backlog below describes the features currently under consideration, but this will change as I get feedback from the testers.

The current release of the game is very short, but demonstrates the basic functionalities that will present in the full game. It also has a very simple plot, with three different endings. See if you can find them all!

Feature backlog:

A proper plot, in which the chicken sexer gradually grows disillusioned with his work, and leads an army of chickens in rebellion.

The possibility of training chickens to perform various tricks, which may be necessary for puzzle solving.

'The Antient Fraternity of Chicken Sexers.' A silly secret society, which will play a pivotal role in the plot. The player will need to advance through various secret rituals to gain access to chicken sexing secrets, and jobs.

Randomized chicken sexing missions. Sex as many chickens as possible before time runs out! It may be necessary to make a certain amount of money this way to advance the plot.

Puzzles revolving around the sexer's need to keep his

fingernails expertly trimmed.

'The Sexy Chick - The Premier Magazine for Chicken Sexers'. Pdf feelie of a chicken sexing magazine, consisting almost entirely of pictures of baby chicks labelled 'Male' or 'Female'. It can possibly also include a short editorial of some kind.

Philosophical discussions about the epistemological consequences of chicken sexing.

Feature suggestions are more than welcome!"

Table of Basic Help Options (continued)

title	subtable	description
"Contacting the author"	--	"Feedback can be sent to: simon@sichris.com"
"Hints"	Table of Hints	--

Table of Hints

title	subtable	description	toggle
"The farmer won't let me sex [the barn chicken]."	Table of Certificate Hints	""	hint toggle rule
"How do I get [the barn chicken] to calm down?"	Table of Calming Hints	""	hint toggle rule
"How do I save [the barn chicken]?"	Table of Saving Hints	""	hint toggle rule

Table of Certificate Hints

hint	used

"You need to prove to the farmer that you know what you are doing."a number

"Do you have any official proof of your credentials?"

"Show the certificate to the farmer."

Table of Calming Hints

hint   used

"There are many ways you can make [the barn chicken] calm down. Try to experiment a bit."   a number

"You can talk to [it-them of the barn chicken], pet [it-them of the barn chicken], or sing a song."

Table of Saving Hints

hint   used

"The farmer doesn't want male chickens."   a number

"If you identify [the barn chicken] as female, you will buy [it-them of the barn chicken] some time."

"You can also try to attack the farmer."

"You aren't much of a fighter. Maybe you can get someone else to do your dirty work for you?"

"You can give commands to other people or animals by typing something like NPC, ACTION."

"Tell [the barn chicken] to attack the farmer."

"You won't be able to command [the barn chicken] until [it-they of the barn chicken] has been both sexed and named."

Part 2 - Scenes

When play begins:

say "[bold type]'Chicken sexing is a delicate art, requiring Zen-like concentration and a brain surgeon's dexterity. The bird is cradled in the left hand and given a gentle squeeze that causes it to evacuate its intestines... With his thumb and forefinger, the sexer flips the bird over and parts a small flap on its hindquarters to expose the cloaca, a tiny vent where both the genitals and anus are situated, and peers deep inside.'

Joshua Foer - 'Moonwalking with Einstein'[roman type]

Another day, another farmer in need of assistance. If it weren't for people like you, the entire American agricultural sector would've gone bankrupt years ago.

You adjust your tie as you step out of the helicopter. Time to get to work.

[bold type]Type ABOUT or HELP for some basic information about the game, as well as a hint menu[roman type].".

Chapter 1 - Simple Scenes

Part 3 - Game World

Chapter 1 - The Barn

The Barn is a room. The description of the barn is "There are piles of hay everywhere in here. A soft layer of sawdust covers the floor, and makes moving around feel like walking through coarse sand. The sun shines through the slits between the planks, causing crisscrossing rays of light to illuminate the dusty air."

The printed name of the barn is "The Barn"

The hay is scenery in the barn. Understand "pile/piles" as the hay.

Instead of doing something to the hay:
        say "You have no particular interest in hay. In fact, you prefer to avoid it."

The light is scenery in the barn. Understand "sun", "dust/dusty" and "sunlight" as the light. The description of the light is "The sunlight illuminating the dusty air gives the place a weird dreamlike quality."

Instead of doing something other than examining to the light:
        say "That's hardly tangible."

The sawdust is scenery in the barn. The description of the sawdust is "Your feet sink into the sawdust. It feels almost like walking on sand.".

Instead of doing something other than examining to the sawdust:
        say "It's just sawdust."

The planks are scenery in the barn. The description of the planks is "The barn is composed of old-fashioned wooden planks."

Instead of doing something other than examining to the planks:
        say "You are a chicken sexer, not a barn architect."

The barn door is a door. It is south of the barn. Understand "Gate/gates/doors" as the barn door. The barn door is scenery and locked.

Instead of exiting when in the barn:
        try going south.

The description of the barn door is "A large pair of wooden doors block the exit from the barn."

Instead of opening the barn door:
        say "You can't leave until you've done your job."

The table is an object in the barn. The description of the table is "A sturdy wooden table."

Instead of taking the table, say "It's much too heavy, and it doesn't belong to you anyway."

Rule for writing a paragraph about the table:
        say "In the middle of the room is a large wooden table, on which [if the chicken is not calm]a baby chick is currently trying to hide between its own tiny wings[otherwise][the barn chicken] is sitting[end if]."

The barn chicken is a chicken on the table. The description of the barn chicken is "A tiny baby chick[if the chicken is not calm], trying to hide in the middle of the empty table[end if].".

The barn chicken can be calm. The barn chicken is not calm.

Instead of taking the chicken when the chicken is neuter:
say "Your job is to sex it, not take it."

Instead of taking the chicken:
say "The farmer is watching you carefully. There is no way you can take [the barn chicken] without being noticed."

Instead of sexing the barn chicken when the farmer is not satisfied:
say "'Hold it right there, buddy,' says the farmer. 'I ain't lettin['] you touch my chickens, until you've shown me you're qualified.'".

Instead of sexing the barn chicken when the farmer is satisfied and the barn chicken is not calm:
say "[The barn chicken] is too nervous. You need to make it calm down before you can do an accurate sexing."

After sexing the chicken:
say "You carefully pick up the chicken with your expertly trimmed fingernails, and inspect its cloaca. In simple cases, the cloaca contains a small bead, the shape of which determines the gender. This is not one of those cases. To almost everyone in the world this would be just another chicken cloaca. To you, it's clearly male.

Now that you know his gender, he somehow seems more

like an individual. You almost feel like you should [bold type]name the chicken something[roman type]."

Instead of talking to the barn chicken when the barn chicken is not calm:

       say "'There, there,' you say, in the soothing voice you have spent years perfecting. 'It'll be over in a second.'

The chicken peeks out from beneath its wings. After a while, it seems to decide that you aren't so dangerous after all, and emerges completely. It looks up at you with big innocent eyes.";

       now the barn chicken is calm.

Instead of talking to the barn chicken when the barn chicken is calm:

       say "You already made [it-them of the barn chicken] calm down. Having an actual conversation is a bit beyond your skills."

Understand "pet [something]" as touching.

Instead of touching the barn chicken when the barn chicken is not calm:

       try talking to the barn chicken.

Instead of singing when the barn chicken is not calm:

       say "'There, there little chiiiicken,' you gently croon. 'Eeeeverything's fine.'

To your surprise, it seems to work. The chicken peeks out from beneath its wings. After a while, it seems to decide that

you aren't so dangerous after all, and emerges completely. It looks up at you with big innocent eyes.";
now the barn chicken is calm.

Instead of singing when the barn chicken is calm:
say "There is no reason to sing."

Instead of touching the barn chicken when the barn chicken is calm:
say "You gently caress the feathers of [the barn chicken]. [It-they of the barn chicken] doesn't seem to mind."

Instead of the barn chicken attacking the farmer when the chickname of the barn chicken is "chicken":
say "The chicken looks at you with big uncomprehending eyes. You can hardly expect a simple animal to understand instructions.";
the rule succeeds.

Instead of the barn chicken attacking the farmer:
say "'[barn chicken],' you say with a confident voice. You raise your finger and point at the farmer: 'Attack!'.

[The barn chicken] slowly stands up, looking like he might fall over at any moment. Then, almost faster than the eye can follow, he launches himself off the table, gliding through the air like a flying squirrel, towards the farmer. He lands on the farmers face and pecks at the eyes, furiously.

The farmer drops to his knees and screams. 'Aaargghhh! Not my vitreous humor! Get off me!' He rips [the barn chicken] off his face and throws him at you. 'You're insane, both of you! Take that damn chicken and get off my farm!

You catch [the barn chicken] in your outstretched hand. 'You're the boss,' you say to the farmer, and shrug. The sunlight caresses your face, as you step outside. It's going to be a wonderful day.

You are never hired as a chicken sexer again, but that's okay. You have [the barn chicken], and all the other chickens you manage to rescue during the next years. The neighbors start avoiding your house. They tell stories about the crazy chicken person, who lives in a house full of chickens, and talks to them all day long. It's fine. Who cares what they think?";
    end the story saying "You've made a difference".

The farmer is a man in the barn. Understand "man" as the farmer. The description of the farmer is "You've met almost as many farmers as chickens, and this one doesn't stand out. He is wearing overalls, a short-sleeved shirt, and a straw hat. He is giving you the usual 'Does this city-slicker really think he knows more about my chickens than I do?' look.".

The farmer is wearing the farmer's clothes. Understand "overalls", "short-sleeved", "shirt", "straw" and "hat" as the farmer's clothes.

The description of the farmer's clothes is "Typical farmer clothes. Not really your style."

Instead of doing something other than examining to the farmer's clothes:
    say "They're not really your style."

Rule for writing a paragraph about the farmer:
say "The farmer stands by the gate to the south, waiting for you to do your job."

Instead of sexing the farmer:
say "He is either male or gender nonconforming. Your training only covered chickens."

The farmer can be satisfied. The farmer is not satisfied.

Instead of talking to the farmer when the farmer is not satisfied:
say "'You better show me some credentials, buddy,' says the farmer."

Instead of talking to the farmer when the farmer is satisfied and the barn chicken is neuter:
say "'Go ahead,' says the farmer, and gestures towards the chicken. 'Show me what you can do.'"

Instead of talking to the farmer when the barn chicken is not neuter and the chickname of the barn chicken is "chicken":
say "You consider telling the farmer that your work is done, but you feel like something is missing. That cute little chicken needs a name."

Instead of showing the certificate to the farmer when the farmer is not satisfied:
say "The farmer reads the certificate and snorts. 'Zen-Nippon school, eh? Well ain't that just swell. Okay, buddy, show me what you've got.'";

now the farmer is satisfied.

Instead of showing the certificate to the farmer when the farmer is satisfied:
    say "He's already seen it."

Instead of giving the certificate to the farmer:
    try showing the certificate to the farmer.

Instead of attacking the farmer when the chickname of the barn chicken is "chicken":
    say "You are not going to attack the farmer for the sake of some nameless chicken."

Instead of attacking the farmer:
    say "You consider trying to take down the farmer for [the barn chicken]'s sake, but decide against it. He looks much stronger than you.

You look at [the barn chicken], and imagine that you see a flash of anger in his eyes. Your mind must be playing tricks on you."

The greeting of the farmer is hello.

Table of Quip Texts (continued)
    quip   quiptext
    hello   "'That didn't take long,' says the farmer, and eyes you suspiciously. 'Which is it then: Male or female?'"
    sayMale   "The farmer smiles, revealing rows of yellow teeth. 'I guess ya won't be givin['] me any eggs, will ya?' He picks up [the barn chicken] from the table, and turns

towards you. 'Let's get to work. Plenty more where that came from.'

With that, he throws the gate wide open, and leaves the barn. You try not to think about [the barn chicken]. It's just a chicken, after all. Plenty more where that came from."

sayFemale "The farmer looks disappointed. 'Really? I coulda sworn it had the swagger of a cockerel. Well, I guess ya'll be givin['] me plenty of eggs, little chicken.' He picks up [the barn chicken] from the table, and turns towards you. 'Let's get to work. Plenty more where that came from.'

With that, he throws the gate wide open, and leaves the barn.

You think about [the barn chicken], and smile. It'll be several weeks at least before the secondary sex characteristics start becoming apparent, even to the untrained eye of the farmer. Several weeks of life for little [barn chicken]. Not much, but better than nothing."

plead "'Hahahaha.' The farmer laughs and drops of spittle land on your face. 'You sure are a funny guy, buddy. Now, which is it: Male or female?'"

The litany of the farmer is the Table of Farmer Conversation.

Table of Farmer Conversation

prompt	response	enabled
"Male"	sayMale	1
"Female"	sayFemale	1
"Does it matter? Can't you just let it live a full life,		

regardless? If it turns out to be male, I'm sure it'll be of use elsewhere..."   plead   1

After quipping when the current quip is sayMale:
      end the story saying "You are a monster"

After quipping when the current quip is sayFemale:
      end the story saying "You made a difference"

In the barn is a reminder.

Rule for writing a paragraph about the reminder:
      say "Your job is to [bold type]sex the chicken[roman type].";
      remove the reminder from play.

ABOUT THE AUTHOR

Simon Christiansen is a writer, poet, and game designer living in Denmark. His stories have been published in a variety of literary journals, and he has written award-winning works of interactive fiction. He is the recipient of three Xyzzy awards for interactive fiction and has been shortlisted for the Niels Klim award for best Danish science fiction novelette.

When not writing, he enjoys reading, juggling, and walking. Visit his website at www.sichris.com.

www.ingramcontent.com/pod-product-compliance
Lightning Source LLC
LaVergne TN
LVHW091621170726
843492LV00007B/2533